For Jamie, my better half

BLOOMSBURY CHILDREN'S BOOKS
Bloomsbury Publishing Inc., part of Bloomsbury Publishing Plc
1385 Broadway, New York, NY 10018

BLOOMSBURY, BLOOMSBURY CHILDREN'S BOOKS, and the Diana logo are trademarks of Bloomsbury Publishing Plc

First published in the United States of America in November 2020
by Bloomsbury Children's Books

Bloomsbury books may be purchased for business or promotional use. For information on bulk purchases please contact Macmillan
Corporate and Premium Sales Department at specialmarkets@macmillan.com

Library of Congress Cataloging-in-Publication Data
available upon request
ISBN 978-1-5476-0424-1 (hardcover) • ISBN 978-1-5476-0425-8 (e-book) • ISBN 978-1-5476-0426-5 (e-PDF)

Art made with charcoal, crayon, and ink and then colored digitally
Book design by Jacob Grant and John Candell
Typeset in Brandon Grotesque
Printed in China by Leo Paper Products, Heshan, Guangdong
2 4 6 8 10 9 7 5 3 1

All papers used by Bloomsbury Publishing Plc are natural, recyclable products made from wood grown in well-managed forests.
The manufacturing processes conform to the environmental regulations of the country of origin.

To find out more about our authors and books visit www.bloomsbury.com and sign up for our newsletters.

Bear Meets Bear

JACOB GRANT

BLOOMSBURY
CHILDREN'S BOOKS

NEW YORK LONDON OXFORD NEW DELHI SYDNEY

Bear was waiting.

He and Spider had ordered a new teapot,
and it would arrive at their house that day.

"It's always great fun to expect a delivery,"
said Bear.

When the doorbell rang, Bear was greeted by a delivery person he had never met before.

"Package for Bear. Please sign here," said Panda.

Bear had never met such a charming lady bear. His heart beat fast.

Bear wanted to say hello. He wanted to say something clever, or funny, or anything at all. But Bear's mouth would not move.

"Please sign for your delivery," she said again.

Eventually Bear signed his name.
He stood there as Panda jumped on
her delivery bike.

He stood there as she pedaled away.
He stood there, nearly dropping the teapot.
Spider found it all rather funny.

Bear dashed across the room.
"One teapot is nice," said Bear.
"But wouldn't two teapots be nicer?"

Spider chuckled. He knew his friend was ordering another teapot to see Panda again. Silly Bear!

Once more, Bear was waiting.
"I wonder if the teapot could
arrive today."

"I am sure today is the day."

"Perhaps I should order another?"

"Oh! She's here!"

But when he saw Panda, Bear was speechless once again.
Spider felt sorry for his friend.

Spider felt less sorry when he saw Bear ordering another teapot.
And another. And each time Bear watched Panda walk away,
without a word.

Spider encouraged Bear to talk to Panda.
To invite her to tea. To at least remember
to breathe, and to stop flooding their
home with teapots.

Bear nodded. "I promise, Spider.
This will be my final order. I am ready."

And for one last time,
Bear waited.

But Bear was not ready for the unpleasant surprise the next morning.

"You're not . . . Panda," whimpered Bear.

The gruff raccoon
shrugged.

"Sign here."

Bear's heart hurt.

"I will never see Panda.
I will never talk to Panda.
And what am I going to do
with so many teapots?!"

There was little Spider could do
to cheer up his friend.

Except, maybe one thing.

Spider ventured out to find the lady bear himself.

He asked everyone he knew if they had seen
Panda, but Spider was not having much luck.

Until he arrived at Duck's house.

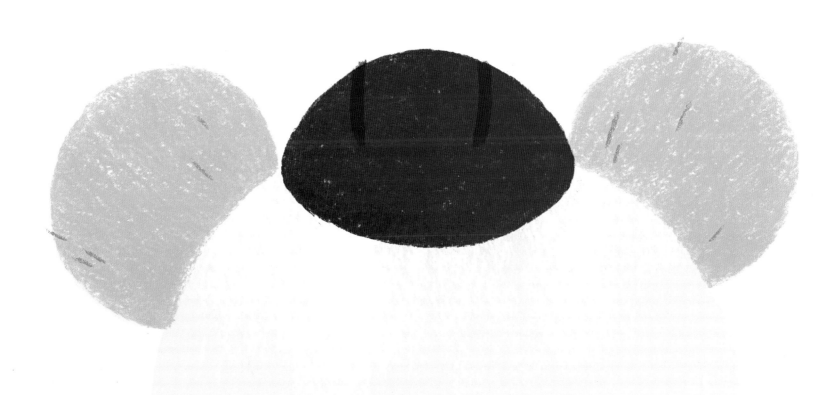

The next day, Bear leaped when he saw his visitor. "Hi. Or, hello again," said Panda. "Your friend passed along your invite to tea."

Bear felt his heart thumping. He felt his body freezing up.
Bear looked at Spider and took a deep breath.
"Tea! Of course, of course. One moment, please."

After some quick tidying of teapots,
Bear welcomed Panda into his home.

It wasn't long before the two bears were chatting and laughing over tea and cookies. Spider was proud to see Bear finally acting himself.

"It was delightful talking with you," said Panda. "Can you believe that most people I deliver to don't say a word to me?" Bear smiled as Panda went on her way.

"Thank you for helping me, Spider. She is very nice,"
said Bear. "But Panda and I will not be meeting
for tea again."

"Panda doesn't like tea!" Bear chuckled.
"I mean, really! Everyone loves a cup of tea.
What could be better than that?"

Bear found it all rather funny.